DIXIE OF DOVER

A Boy and Dog Story

DIXIE OF DOVER

A BOY AND DOG STORY

by

JEAN POINDEXTER COLBY

Illustrated by Mary Stevens

LITTLE, BROWN and COMPANY
Boston · Toronto

Books by Jean Poindexter Colby

PETER PAINTS THE U.S.A.

JENNY

JIM THE CAT

DIXIE OF DOVER

A Boy and Dog Story

Published simultaneously in Canada
by Little, Brown & Company (Canada) Limited

PRINTED IN THE UNITED STATES OF AMERICA

DIXIE OF DOVER

A Boy and Dog Story

To my daughter Jeannie, who has helped
so much in this book and lots of others

I

DIXIE was a very fine Welsh Terrier with a pedigree as long as he himself was short. He came from a well-known kennel on Long Island where the owner bred Welsh Terriers as a specialty. This kennel was very clean and looked just like a modern hospital. Each dog had his own little stall with his name over it in gold letters. There was a framed pedigree beside the name, and then over both hung the ribbons that each dog had won at dog shows.

When this story starts Dixie was so little that he had no ribbons as yet, but his mother's and father's cages were covered

with them. And he had a most impressive pedigree*. Here
it is:

		Ch. Strathglass	Ch. Galen Arsen of Marlu
Dixie	Ch. Strathglass of Wyncote (Sire)		Ch. Vaynor Perky of Marlu
		Ch. Strathglass Dyma	Fencliffe Welsh Emblem
			Iechyd Da
	Ch. Mawr Hydi (Dam)	Brennin	Aman Ace of Halcyon
			Aman Anita of Halcyon
		Dyma Fi	Aman Supreme
			Blodyn Glan

You can see that his family line really does go back to Wales
to his great-grandsire, who was one of several Welsh Terriers
used on a large manor farm to hunt — especially otters — and
to drive the cattle and sheep and guard the flocks. In spite
of their small size these little dogs are used for these purposes
because they are so intelligent and so courageous. Also, their
coats grow long and shaggy in winter, giving them such
warmth and protection that they can stay out in cold weather
and freezing storms better than almost any other breed.

* This is a fictitious pedigree, made up of various champion Welsh Terriers.

These qualities of courage and endurance were really what made Lieutenant John Reed, called "Dixie" for his Southern accent, pick out a little Welsh Terrier from the kennel on Long Island. He wanted him as a gift for the ten-year-old son of his superior officer, Captain Converse Montgomery, who had saved his life in the South Pacific. Every year since the war, Lieutenant Reed had sent his captain some sort of gift but not until the previous year had he been able to present it himself at the Montgomery home in Dover, Massachusetts.

The soldier had been given a warm welcome by Mrs. Montgomery and the two children, but his happiness was dimmed because his old war buddy was not able to join in. A blood infection picked up in the South Pacific had grown worse and the Captain lay in a veterans' hospital nearby, without much chance of recovery.

As far as Lieutenant Reed could see, Mrs. Montgomery was managing the big house all right alone. Katy O'Brien, the cook, was still there but Keith MacPhersen, the Scot who had been gardener, chauffeur and nursemaid rolled into one, had been dismissed for reasons of economy. Mrs. Montgomery didn't "need" him, she said, but Dixie thought it would be a lonely place without a man or a dog.

This is why he sent up the tiny Welsh terrier puppy to ten-year-old Gerry Montgomery after his visit. "Every boy needs a dog," he had said to Mrs. Montgomery — and he had added to himself, "And you certainly need one here."

The little Welsher arrived in a beautiful traveling box especially made for shipping dogs. The Railway Express man carried it into the front hall, where Gerry was jumping up and down with eagerness.

"I want one Gershom Converse Montgomery the Third," the man announced firmly. "And where would the gentleman with that long name be?" he asked.

"Right here," answered Gerry. "I'm that gentleman," he giggled.

"It's a terribly long name for the likes of you," the expressman said. "You've got to sign the whole of it, too, to get this prize package."

At this point the prize package just mentioned began to give out with some strange rustlings and little barks.

"Oh yes, I'll sign it!" cried Gerry, doing so. "Golly, I wish I could open it now! Mother! Katy!" he called to Mrs. Montgomery, who was coming down the staircase, and to Katy, who had appeared from the back hall. "How do you open this trunk? What kind of a dog is it?"

The expressman dropped on his knees beside the box. "I'll open it for you. He's a cute one, as I know, being as how I fed him myself. But I don't know for the life of me what kind he is."

With that he opened a little door in the end of the box and out wiggled the puppy. He flung himself on Gerry and then on Mrs. Montgomery, dancing around in circles with joy at getting out of the box. "It's a Welsh Terrier from Dixie to you," Mrs. Montgomery declared with delight. "I remember Dixie mentioned that breed as being good watchdogs."

"Oh, Mother, he's perfect!" Gerry cried. "Dixie was so nice to send him. What shall I name him?"

"Well, don't be after calling him by that mouthful of a name of yours, for he won't come until Christmas." The expressman gathered up his slips and pencil. "What about that name you just said, Dixie? It would be proper to name him after the man who gave him to you. Well, I'll be off now. Have a good time with him!"

"Good-by, and thank you," Gerry and his mother called after him, then bent their attention to the puppy again.

"Dixie *would* be a good dog name, wouldn't it, Mother?" Gerry looked up at her.

"Yes, it would," she agreed. "Not very Welsh, but Dixie Reed would be so pleased. How about Dixie of Dover for his kennel name? See, look at his pedigree. One of his ancestors is Aman Ace of Halcyon. And his father is Champion Strathglass of Wyncote." She read slowly from the paper she had taken from a small envelope tied to the box.

"Goodness, those names are hard to pronounce!" Gerry's fourteen-year-old sister Barbara arrived on the scene. "Are they English or what?"

"Welsh — just the way *your* name is English," said Mrs. Montgomery.

"Dixie of Dover is easy to say," Gerry commented. "Let's call him that. I like that."

"So do I," agreed both his mother and sister at once.

So Dixie of Dover it was, and out into the sunshine the boy and the dog went, capering around each other with joy.

II

THE NEXT WEEKS were full of fun for both boy and dog. Dixie soon learned that he must guard the fifteen acres which belonged to the Montgomerys. He patrolled the long drive that led up to the house and questioned every arrival in his brisk puppy way. He soon learned just who should rightly come up the drive — the milkman, the laundry-man, the oil heater truck, and especially Keith MacPhersen, the former gardener. Keith had bought part ownership in a gas station with the money he had saved from his wages. In spite of his work he came regularly to see the Montgomerys, to inquire after the health of the captain, and to look over the place to see if all was well.

He was delighted with the little terrier. "He's a fine dog, that Welsher. I'm a Scotsman myself and a great collie man, but I know how the Welsh value these dogs. And he's a very good one of his breed. Gerry, you and I will give him a little obedience training this spring and then enter him in the Hunt Club Horse and Dog Show this June. He'll have to be plucked first, though."

Gerry ran to tell his mother this news. "What is plucking, Mother? Does it hurt a dog? Will we have to do it to Dixie to show him in the Dog Show?"

Mrs. Montgomery looked thoughtful. "Yes, I think we will but I'm sure it doesn't hurt — and anyway he would be uncomfortable in that heavy coat this summer. Wales is a cool mountainous country and these dogs are equipped by nature for that climate."

So when June arrived and the children got out of school, Barbara helped Gerry give Dixie a bath and then the whole family took him to a nearby kennel to be plucked.

Afterwards he looked so handsome! The clipping brought out the fine lines of his head, his compact body and his sturdy legs. As is customary with Welsh Terriers, the clipper left him with longish eyebrows that stuck straight out and gave him a very "casual" look, Barbara said. The hair was also left long on his lower legs, and Gerry loved these funny "fur pants."

10

On the day of the Dog Show, they bathed him again, put his pedigree in a folder, and brought out the new green leash they had bought for the occasion.

It had been agreed that Gerry would show his own dog, so they went early for him to see how the other handlers showed their dogs.

It wasn't a very big affair. There were only three other Welsh Terriers, so they entered Dixie also in the general Terrier Class and in the general Puppy Class.

When it came time to show him, both puppy and Gerry were so excited they could hardly keep still. But Dixie's careful training by Keith had taken hold and he stood beautifully for the judges in all three events.

Gerry handled him well, too, and deserved his share of the three rosettes they brought home that afternoon: a blue, or First Place, in the Puppy Class; a red, or Second Place, in the Welsh Terrier Class; and a white, or Third Place, in the Terrier Class. This was a good showing considering there were some very fine dogs there, especially in the big Terrier Class.

"Bring him around next year, young fellow," one of the judges said. "He'll be grown then and will really walk off with the prizes. He is of championship stock."

The Montgomery family were more than satisfied with the results of their first dog show and had a suitable celebration

when they got home. It took the form of a steak dinner with
French fried potatoes, salad from the garden, and chocolate
ice cream with fudge sauce from the store. Dixie growled
and yipped with pleasure over the big steak bone with lots
of meat left on it that was his share of the feast. And afterwards he quickly demolished the fine ribbon tied on his collar
by rolling gaily over and over out in the hayfield until it was
nothing but shreds.

The whole family laughed and chatted at the table as they

reviewed the events of the show and all went to bed with joy in their hearts over this charming addition to their family.

Their pleasure was short-lived, however, for the very next day Mrs. Montgomery was called over to the hospital, where her husband had taken a turn for the worse. There followed weeks of daily and then twice-daily visits, and one hot day in July came the dread news that the young war hero was dead.

Mrs. Montgomery bore up bravely during the funeral and the sad days that followed. Barbara and Gerry helped their mother all they could, but their hearts were heavy and they often wandered around their beautiful place forlornly, thinking of their beloved father and wondering what was going to happen now that he was gone.

They knew, for instance, that there wasn't much money left. Because Mr. Montgomery had been a soldier, the government took care of the hospital expenses and would pay Mrs. Montgomery quite a pension besides. But this would not be enough to cover the expenses of their big place, much less pay for food, clothes, heat and schooling. Because the Montgomerys lived so far out in the country, the children went to private schools. These were dismissed for the summer, but both Barbara and Gerry worried about the fall and the possibility of getting up at six o'clock to go on the bus way across the county to the overcrowded school in Harrison.

But it turned out they would not be going to the Harrison school. After a month of seeing lawyers and other advisers, Mrs. Montgomery held a family meeting and explained the financial situation to her son and daughter. Dixie of Dover was also present and seemed to listen as if he too understood and sympathized.

The Montgomery family was not too badly off, their mother explained. But they had to cut down on living costs and it seemed only sensible to sell the big place and move to something less expensive to keep up. Their Grandfather Montgomery, she continued, had owned several houses in Boston and Brookline which had been bringing in rent and would continue to do so, but there was one house in particular that hadn't been modernized and hence was hard to rent even to roomers. It had been a good house in its day and, even though the neighborhood had gone down, it was still a comfortable old place with a big yard and nice trees.

It was Mrs. Montgomery's idea that they move in there after they sold the Dover place. The children agreed at once. They were anxious to support their mother in this time of need but sick at heart at leaving their home where they had both been born and brought up.

III

THE FOLLOWING MONTH was the hardest that
Gerry and Barbara had ever known. It was even hard on
Dixie, who had become official guardian of the big place.

He could not understand the sudden flow of cars and people
up the driveway and through the house and grounds — people
he had never seen before, objectionable, prying people who
looked in closets and bedrooms and even poked under rugs
and drilled holes in the beams in the basement.

He almost flew at a boy who pranced up to Gerry and said,
"I'm going to have your room and I'm going to mark up all
that fancy wallpaper, and bust up your bird feeder, and grind
a hole in that workbench."

Fortunately Mrs. Montgomery did not have to sell to the family this boy belonged to, but there came the dreaded day when the house really was sold. The people who bought it were very well-behaved and quiet and their one little girl had the generosity to say to Barbara, "My, you must hate to leave this lovely place. Come back any time you want to. I'd love to have you."

This made Barbara rush to the kitchen to put her head on Katy's plump shoulder and cry and cry. But after a while even she agreed that it was better to have nice people own the place as long as they had to sell it.

It was late one August day that they all drove into Brookline to see the old house they were going to live in. It was very hot outside and the children were astonished when their mother turned the big key in the lock and a wave of cool air rushed out to greet them.

"These old houses are cool in summer because their walls are thick and the ceilings are so high," Mother explained.

"And because they're so dark," Barbara added, peering into the gloom.

"Now wait a minute, me girl," objected Katy as she went ahead and pulled up the shades on the long windows. "Oh my!" she gasped in dismay as the long rays of sunlight revealed dark gloomy woodwork and wallpaper peeling off in great strips.

"Don't be discouraged," Mrs. Montgomery put in quickly. "We have enough money to paint and paper the whole house and I think you will find these big rooms very pretty and comfortable then."

"There's a marble fireplace in every room!" called Gerry, who had darted ahead. "Even in the dining room. Won't it be fun to have a fire at dinnertime in the winter?"

"And at breakfast, too," his mother added gently. "When I was a little girl, that is when a fire seemed the best to me — a cheery, warm way to start the day. I grew up in a house very like this one."

Her memories were interrupted by a yell from Barbara, who had gone upstairs and was looking around. "Wait until you see! Come quick! This bathroom is really something!"

Gerry and Dixie dashed upstairs at top speed, followed more slowly by Mrs. Montgomery and Katy. Gerry too let out a yell. "Oh, Mom, this you've got to see! The bathtub is as big as a house and is in a big dark polished box! Gee, isn't it beautiful! I bet I could lie down in it" — and to demonstrate he got in and did. There was a foot or more to spare, which was soon taken up by Dixie, who leaped right in after him.

"And look, Mother, there's a china basin!" Barbara was dancing up and down in delight. "Isn't it gorgeous? Isn't it

regal! And look at the rose painted on the bottom of the bowl!"

"That isn't the only place there are roses," smiled Mother. "Look at the toilet bowl!" And sure enough at the bottom of that was a big red rose, too. "You see, in the early nineteen-hundreds there was a rage for hand-painted china and it extended even to plumbing fixtures. These fixtures came from Limoges, a city in France that was famous for its hand-painted china."

"Praises be!" said Katy. "I never saw the like. Why haven't the roses been scrubbed off in all these years?"

"The same reason the pattern hasn't been scrubbed off our china even though we wash it three times a day," Mrs. Montgomery explained. "Anyway the main thing is that all this plumbing works perfectly, the man said, so we don't have to worry about that. Now let's look at the bedrooms."

Even the children could not help but admire the big airy rooms and could see that with paint and papering they would be very livable. Gerry and Dixie bobbed around through the house, into every nook and cranny, and finally found the back stairs. They clattered down them and soon another whoop came from Gerry and a frightened bark from Dixie.

"Mother, oh Mother, wait until you see the stove! It's a monster, Mother, and the kitchen is as big as our dining room in Dover."

Mother and Katy entered the kitchen from the pantry door, and Mother's face was troubled as she looked at Katy.

"The saints preserve us and keep us, look at that black creature!" Katy's hands flew up and her mouth dropped open.

"Oh, we'll surely get a new stove, Katy," Mrs. Montgomery hastened to say.

"A new stove? With that great black thing ready to deliver the goods? That's like the stove my mother used to cook on for many a long year in South Boston. I know how to tame the creature. Sure and you wait and see the pies and cakes and roasts and bread I can coax out of that one. And you can keep your kettle simmering on the back of it and not have to light the gas all the time. And it's elegant for soups and especially to put your feet in the oven of a cold winter's day. A new stove, I wouldn't have it!"

"I'm not sure I could work it, though, Katy." Mrs. Montgomery shook her head. "We always had a gas stove even when I was a little girl."

"Sure and I'll teach you how. And when you have it under control you won't want anything different. Anyway I'll be home to cook your dinner. All you'll worry about is lunch. And I can leave that hot in yonder oven when I go out."

Barbara, Gerry and Dixie suddenly turned and stared at Katy. It was Barbara who spoke: "You're not going, Katy! Not you, too?"

21

Katy turned to face them, her hands on her hips. "Now what are you two doing, worrying up a new worry when we've got enough real ones? Your mother's friend Mr. Dillon, who has taken you all to his restaurant many a time, he has offered me a job as part-time cook so I can give his friends the good old Irish dishes for luncheon. He is going to make a special of them or something. Anyway your mother, she was after saying she couldn't afford to have me here but I told her I had to have a place to lay my head. So I'm going to live with you same as always, cook your breakfasts and dinner on yonder demon, but go out for luncheon with Sassiety!" Whereupon she laughed a big laugh and the children joined in, their relief showing on their faces.

"Now take yourselves off, you two!" Katy waved her hand at Gerry and Barbara. "Show the little Welshman the yard and tell him to guard it. We may need him when I think of all the people as must be living in those tenements nearby."

So off the two children and the little dog went to explore. Mrs. Montgomery and Katy remained in the kitchen, making notes on necessary changes, peering into cupboards and talking things over.

Suddenly a scratching noise and a thumping seemed to come from a big built-in series of oak doors. "Glory be, it's ghosts we have, too!" cried Katy, her face white as a piece of paper.

"It comes from over here," Mrs. Montgomery declared as

she crossed the room and pulled open one of the doors. All
of six inches thick, it swung slowly out, revealing Gerry and
Dixie sitting all crouched together in a metal-lined compart-
ment.

"Oh, it's one of those big old iceboxes." Mrs. Montgomery
signed with relief but her face was stern. "How did you get
in?" she asked of the boy and the dog.

"There's a little door on the outside of the house that
opened when I unlatched it," Gerry explained in a puzzled
tone. "So we just scrambled in to see where it went."

"In the old days the iceman put the ice in through that door. It closed on you, didn't it?" his mother said, eyeing him.

"Yes, it did," Gerry admitted.

"And if Katy and I hadn't happened to be in the kitchen, you couldn't have gotten out, could you?" she persisted.

"No," the boy replied, "but you *were* here. And I'm out."

Mrs. Montgomery's tone relaxed. "Yes, thank goodness, you are, but you've just been in one of the most dangerous places a child could be. So many children have been suffocated in old iceboxes — most of them have been thrown away on city dumps — that now many towns and cities make it a law that the front doors of all refrigerators must be taken off before they are thrown out. And that is one thing we'll do right away — or rather, we'll nail that outside door closed. I'll ask Keith to do it the next time he comes. But until then you must stay out of there. Do you understand?"

Gerry's mother hardly ever spoke to him so abruptly, and tears began to come into the boy's eyes. Dixie seemed to sense his unhappiness and ran over to lick his hand. Then he trotted over to Mrs. Montgomery and laid a paw on her dress, looking up at her so meaningfully that she said, "Did I speak too harshly, Dixie? I'm sorry, Gerry. Run out and play now. We have to be serious about serious things, though. I'm sure you agree with me."

24

"I do, Mother. That was a wonderful place to hide but I don't want to suffocate and neither does Dixie. Anyway there are lots of other places around here. Come on, Dix!" And off they went, banging the old screen door to as they left.

Peace settled once more in the big kitchen but only for a moment. A wild barking suddenly came from outside. It was Dixie frenziedly objecting to someone or something.

Mrs. Montgomery and Katy rushed to the window just in time to see two boys drop down into the yard from the high stone wall that surrounded the acre or more of land that went with the house.

In less than no time Dixie had them backed up against the wall, dancing around them, barking furiously, creating an uproar that would have done credit to a Great Dane.

"Oh dear, Dixie shouldn't do that!" Mrs. Montgomery wrung her hands. "I suppose those are some of the neighborhood boys."

"And what good would a dog be who would let a pair of rascals like that steal into our place from over our wall?" Katy defended. "They'll have to learn their manners from the start and I'm here to teach them!" With that she threw open the back door, mop in hand, and started across the yard like a warrior about to do battle.

Mrs. Montgomery hesitated a moment and then ran after

her. "Katy, please don't say anything. If we start the wrong way with our neighbors . . ."

But matters had already been taken over by Gerry, who had corralled Dixie and was talking with the boys.

The taller, red-headed one was saying, "Say, you goin' to live in this dump? Nobody has lived here for years. They was goin' to tear it down, my father heard."

"Your father heard wrong." Barbara had come around from behind the barn to her brother's defense.

"Oh, a blonde queen, huh?" the shorter, black-haired boy put in. "We ain't had no blondes lately. Maybe we could use you in our gang."

"You leave my sister alone," Gerry demanded, "or I'll let my dog loose."

At that point Mrs. Montgomery hurried up to them and said softly, "Hello, boys. Do you live around here?"

The red-haired one eyed her and didn't answer. The shorter one said, "Yeah," which he changed, after looking at Katy, to "Yes, ma'am."

"What are your names?" Mrs. Montgomery asked pleasantly, although her voice trembled a little. "I am Mrs. Montgomery and this is Gerry and Barbara Montgomery. And Miss O'Brien." She indicated Katy, who stood with her face set, her mouth one grim line.

"That's my name, too." The older boy suddenly broke his silence. "Isn't that just dandy? Bill O'Brien. Perhaps we're cousins or somethin'," he sneered.

"Young man — " Katy had fire in her eye.

"And what is *your* name?" Mrs. Montgomery turned quickly to the smaller boy.

"I'm Paul Delasapio," the boy answered rather shyly. Then he asked unexpectedly, "What kind of a dog is that? He's awful cute."

"Cute, huh!" the O'Brien boy spoke out of the corner of his mouth. "It would be cute if he'd a taken a piece outa ya. We'd a sued ya if he had." He eyed Mrs. Montgomery belligerently.

Mrs. Montgomery seemed to pay no attention. "You know it's almost noon and I'm hungry. We brought a picnic with us and I'm sure there's enough for two more. Would you two boys like to join us?"

The boys looked at each other in surprise while Katy threw up her hands and marched into the house.

"What'll we do, huh, Paul?" the tall boy asked.

"They ain't going to poison us," Paul replied.

The tall boy spat into some weeds and turned to face Mrs. Montgomery. "Okay, ma'am. It's a deal if ya really mean it."

"I do," Mrs. Montgomery smiled at him. "We'll have it in the shade under that big pine tree."

Paul smiled back and said, "Say, that would be great. My father always brings home some pizza for lunch. There's always enough for a million. I'll go get some. Do you like pizza?"

Mrs. Montgomery nodded her head. "I love it." Whereupon Paul disappeared out the front gate.

"What's pizza?" asked Gerry.

"It's an Italian dish with cheese and tomatoes — it's very good," replied his mother, who was watching Bill O'Brien. The big boy was dragging his sneaker back and forth in the gravel of the drive as if he had something on his mind. "Should you let your mother know you won't be home for lunch, Bill?" she asked.

"My mother ain't home," he answered gruffly. "But I gotta go home and feed the baby. You see," he took a deep breath, "my mother works, my father works, my sister works, my brother works, so I have to take care of the baby. Mrs. Callahan looks in during the morning but I'm supposed to be home now, heatin' up the bottle. I guess I shouldn't come to the picnic. See, I'm supposed ta stay home. Unless . . ." he looked hesitantly at Mrs. Montgomery.

She got the idea. "Why don't you bring the baby?"

29

"Yeah," he accepted eagerly. "Yeah, she'd like it out here. It's hot up at the apartment. We ain't got no trees, nothing like this. But I ain't got nothing to bring to the picnic. No pizzas nor nothing."

"That's all right," put in Barbara unexpectedly, "you have the baby. I'd love to see the baby."

IV

DIXIE seemed relieved when Bill left. He trotted
after him, his hair bristling, nose to the ground, until he came
to the edge of the lawn, and then trotted back slowly to the
group still standing by the wall.

Gerry was saying, "I think he's awful and I don't see why
he talks like that — 'ain't got no trees — ain't got nothin'.'
Why does he talk like that, Mother? Doesn't he go to school?"

Mrs. Montgomery looked thoughtful. "I'm sure he's taught
good English at school, but perhaps he hears it spoken that
way at home, or perhaps his friends speak like that. Sometimes you do what the gang does because you don't want to
be different."

Barbara too had a question. "But he is Irish like Katy, Mother. Yet he doesn't talk with her accent and his words don't sound nice like hers."

"And it's glad I am to hear you say that." Katy herself appeared with the picnic basket. "There's good Irish and bad Irish just as there are good Americans and bad Americans."

Mrs. Montgomery put in gently, "But you're not really Irish, Katy, any more than my children are English."

"Irish? Of course I'm Irish," Katy bristled. "Wasn't my mother an O'Dean of County Cork and my father an O'Brien from Dublin?"

Mrs. Montgomery laughed as she took out the sandwiches and arranged them on paper plates.

"I know, Katy, and you ought to be proud of them. But what are you yourself, and proud of it, too, I hope?"

Katy started to argue but suddenly stopped. "Sure and I know what you mean. It's an American I am just like yourselves." And with that she chuckled and went back into the house.

"But if she is an American, why does she have a brogue — the way Daddy used to say she had? And if she's Irish why dosen't Bill O'Brien talk like her?" Gerry never let a subject die until he understood it thoroughly.

Mrs. Montgomery tried to explain. "Because Katy's father and mother came straight from Ireland here and talked to

Katy with an Irish brogue. Now Bill's father and mother were probably born here, of Irish parents. You see, the longer you stay away from 'the old country,' as they call it, the more *you* talk like the people around you."

Barbara chimed in. "So everybody who is born here, like Katy or Keith or Bill O'Brien, is American no matter how they talk."

"Right," answered Mrs. Montgomery emphatically.

"Even that other boy with the funny name?" Gerry asked. "That Paul . . ."

"Yes, even Paul Delasapio," agreed his mother. "And that isn't a funny name, Gerry — any funnier than Montgomery is to him. His grandparents probably came from Italy, which is a beautiful country, son, and he keeps his Italian-sounding name just as you've kept the English name of Montgomery."

"They still eat Italian food, though," Gerry persisted. "Here he comes with that pizza. I'm not sure I'll like it."

Sure enough, Paul came trotting up the driveway, holding a big pie-shaped object above his head.

"My father said we could have lots of pizza." He smiled at them all. "And he said welcome to this dumpy neighborhood. He and Mamma will come to see you some day."

He put the pizza down on a big tree stump and a delightful aroma filled the air. Both Gerry and Dixie moved over closer. And Mrs. Montgomery too joined the admiring circle.

33

"Dig in, folks," cried Paul, pleased with the reception. "My dad is famous for his pizza. He says it is good for kids. Oh-oh, here comes Bill. He doesn't like it. He calls it Wop food."

Everyone looked around to see Bill O'Brien come stalking up the drive, pushing a rattletrap stroller. In it was a smiling dirty-faced baby, happily sucking on a bottle. Bill's face was rather red with embarrassment but on he pushed resolutely, stopping the carriage in front of Barbara.

"Oh, what a cute baby," she said, but looked away with a slight shudder from the sticky face, the spotted dress and little jam-covered hands.

Mrs. Montgomery came up to stand by Bill. "She is a darling baby, Bill. May I take her a moment and show her to Katy? You help yourself to sandwiches and milk and pizza. It's delicious."

"Me eat that — " But Bill stopped after one look at Mrs. Montgomery and changed his tone. "Okay, okay. I'm sure hungry. I could eat anything."

Mrs. Montgomery went in the house while the children began making inroads on the food. In a little while Katy appeared to hang some suspiciously small clothes on the line in the sun. She cast one baleful look in Bill's direction and slammed back into the house. Barbara chuckled while the boys, undisturbed, went on eating.

"Are you going to come to the Bradford School?" Bill asked

Gerry as he got up to go. This was the school around the corner.

"Yes, I'll be in sixth grade because I'll be eleven in September," Gerry answered proudly.

"Well, don't wear them things." Bill scowled at Gerry's shorts and ankle socks. "The gang'll take you apart."

Gerry sat up very straight. "What's the matter with my clothes? Everybody wore shorts at the school where I went last year."

"Listen, kid, I'm just warnin' ya." Bill stretched and yawned. "Ya wear dungarees, see? All the time, see?"

Gerry stood up, looking very serious. Dixie came anxiously to his side. "I have dungarees, of course," he said, "but my mother won't let me wear them to dinner and anyway these are much cooler in summer."

"Oh," sneered Bill, "so your mother won't let you wear them to dinner. Listen, kid, I'm warnin' ya for the last time and I wouldn't bother with no little squirt except I had good food here and your mother's takin' care of my sister. You wear dungarees, see, and you do what the rest of the guys do or you'll be out of luck in this neck of the woods, see?" Whereupon he trust his face menacingly into Gerry's and raised his fist.

What he was going to do with it no one ever found out because Dixie, seeing a threat to his beloved master, went into

36

action. Straight he jumped for Bill's throat, but Bill drew
back in alarm just enough so that Dixie's teeth fastened instead in the top of the dungarees that Bill had just been rec-
ommending. Around and around the big boy whirled but
Dixie hung fiercely on, growling like a catamount all the
while.

"Call off your dog!" cried Bill. "I ain't goin' to touch ya.
Call off this pooch!"

The uproar brought Mrs. Montgomery and Katy out of the house on the double. "Down, Dixie!" cried Mrs. Montgomery. "Down, boy!"

The dog obeyed but stood by Gerry, growling, and with his hair still on end.

"What's this all about, you spalpeen?" cried Katy to Bill O'Brien. "Don't you know how to act like a gentleman?"

By this time Bill's fear had gone and his confidence returned. "Gentleman yet! Ha! I won't waste my time on you. I was just telling this little *gentleman* if he come to school like that, he'll get roughed up. And a lot of thanks I get for my pains. That crazy pooch trying to tear me apart — " He swung a kick at Dixie and the whole scene would have taken place again had not Paul scooped up Dixie and carried him toward the house.

"He's a cute one and you're not going to hit him!" The dark-haired boy held the little dog close, and to everyone's surprise he seemed to like it. "Go on home, Bill, we were having a good time until you started a row."

"I'll go home, you bet." Bill looked daggers at his friend. "I'll take my sister and go. You can chum around with these stuck-ups if you want to. I ain't goin' to have nuthin' to do with 'em."

"Thank goodness!" cried Katy. "I'll be getting your sister, and good riddance to bad — "

Mrs. Montgomery broke in. "Katy, I'll get the baby. Barbara and I would like to give her to Bill."

Katy turned and went into the house followed by Mrs. Montgomery and Barbara. Paul and Gerry stood patting Dixie while Bill waited alone, bewildered. When Barbara came out carrying the baby, he gasped and turned red.

"You had a nerve," he said, "cleaning her up. She was all right. We ain't snobs." And he put the baby down so hard in the carriage she started to cry. But the swaying of the carriage soon stopped her and they sailed out the drive, Bill pushing as hard as he could and keep his dignity.

V

MR. AND MRS. DELASAPIO came to call the following Sunday afternoon. They were both plump and genial and Mrs. Delasapio was beautiful with lovely black hair and eyes and a peaches-and-cream complexion. She had an especially soft and winning voice. Paul came, too, looking very clean and neat.

Dixie ran to meet them and did not bark as he usually did.

"He remembers an old friend," said Mrs. Montgomery as she greeted them.

The Delasapios were enthusiastic about Dixie, perhaps because Paul showed him off with so much pleasure.

After the introductions were over, Mr. Delasapio said, "Paul has talked about nothing but this Welsh Terrier since he met all of you. He wants a dog very much, but the traffic around here is so bad we won't let him have one."

"We have a little extra land here, or we wouldn't dare keep one either," agreed Mrs. Montgomery. "Dixie rarely goes off the place."

"It is a lovely old place," said Mrs. Delasapio. "We are so glad you have come to live in it. But aren't you worried about being in this neighborhood? It is quite rough, you know. We have been here since we first came from Italy but we don't enjoy it."

Mrs. Montgomery laughed and said, "Oh, we expect to like it here." Then she asked, "Wouldn't you care to see the inside of the house? My husband's parents lived here for many years and we have started to do it over as it was then."

Dixie proudly trotted through all the rooms ahead of them as they marveled at the high ceilings and the scrollwork on them. On one an angel was blowing a horn, right at Gerry's bed. Both the boys thought this was very funny. When they looked at the bathroom, Paul lay out straight in the big bathtub and Dixie jumped in with him and seemed to look up and smile, just as he had with Gerry.

When they returned to the living room, Mrs. Montgomery and Barbara excused themselves to get some lemonade and

cookies, and Barbara couldn't wait for the pantry door to close before she asked:

"Now, Mother, how do *they* speak English so well? They have just come from Italy, at least within the last ten years?"

"Let's ask them," said Mother unexpectedly. "They seem very friendly and look like educated people. They might be interested in what we were talking about."

"Oh, Mother, don't — " wailed Barbara, embarrassed. But her mother had already pushed her way through the swinging door into the dining room with her tray of glasses, and all

Barbara could do was follow with the pitcher of lemonade and the cookies. She arrived in the living room in time to hear her mother say:

"This is quite a change for us from the country to the city, and the children are interested in the people they've met. I have been trying to explain why some of them speak with an accent and some do not. Now you, for instance, speak perfect English even though you were born in Italy. I feel sure that even if we knew Italian very well, we would speak it with an accent in *your* country."

This delighted Mr. Delasapio. "We surprised you, eh?" he laughed. "Well, let me explain that at my school in Milan we had to learn to speak English as well as Italian, and also I studied a year at Boston University Business School before going into the restaurant business. And as to my wife, I am very proud of her. She gave up a fine career as a singer to marry me. Speak good English? If you'll pardon my saying so, she speaks better English than many American-born people!"

The children all laughed and Mrs. Delasapio blushed. Barbara was the one who spoke next. "Oh, Mrs. Delasapio, do you really sing? Would you sing something for us? I like to sing, too. Perhaps you could help me."

So they all gathered around the piano and Mrs. Delasapio's gorgeous voice rose and fell in the rich, full tones of an aria from the opera *Traviata*. They all applauded and then Mrs.

Delasapio asked Barbara to select a song. This she did, "Santa Lucia," but they had hardly started when Dixie threw his head back and whined high and long. Everyone stopped to laugh, but when they started again Dixie started too.

"Oh dear," said Mrs. Montgomery, "Dixie is going to be another singing puppy. When I was a little girl we had an Irish Terrier who always whined when my mother sang 'Holy Night.' He only did it for that one hymn but we finally had to omit it from our Christmas songs!"

So Gerry and Paul took Dixie outside to play and the music proceeded more peacefully. When it was time to go, everyone shook hands, and Mrs. Montgomery said, "You were so nice to come. Do come again."

"Thank you, we will," said Mr. Delasapio. "I'm not sure you'll enjoy this neighborhood but we're glad you are here. We would not stay here ourselves but I like to live near my restaurant and also I can walk home to my wife and boy at lunchtime. You must come and see us."

"Yes," urged his wife, "I will call you. Barbara has a very sweet voice and — "

"So has Dixie!" piped up Gerry, who had appeared for the good-bys.

Mrs. Delasapio reached down and gave Gerry a hug. "Yes, he has. One of his notes was a good high C. I struck that key on the piano just now and it was the same!"

Everyone laughed and Gerry and Dixie saw the Delasapios out the gate.

Soon it was time for school and both Gerry and Barbara were glad to go. The painters and paperhangers were all over the house and the noise and confusion were tremendous. A leak had been discovered in a bedroom, which meant that the old clapboards on that side of the house had to be taken off and new copper flashing put on underneath. So there was hammering all day long combined with the smell of paint and paste. The family could hardly walk anywhere without falling over someone or something, or touch anything without sticking to it.

Gerry had always enjoyed school, so he pranced off the first day full of high spirits. He carefully wore dungarees and a sports shirt, as Bill O'Brien had advised. So he felt right in the gang when Paul Delasapio met him on the steps and introduced him to some of the boys and girls going in. They looked him over rather sharply, especially the boys, but everything went all right until the roll call came. When Gerry stood up and gave his name, Gershom Converse Montgomery III, there were several indignant snorts, a Bronx cheer, and general tittering. The teacher called the class to order and the pupils quieted down, but after Gerry went to the blackboard for his turn at arithmetic, he came back to find the milk for his lunch spilled all over the inside of his desk.

The teacher hurried down the aisle to help him clean it up, but seemed more concerned about the mess than about who had done it.

"You must put your lunch in your locker like the other boys," she scolded.

"I'm sorry. I didn't know," replied Gerry miserably.

"And be sure the cork is tight in your Thermos bottle," Miss Carpenter went on. "Here, take this rag to the janitor."

Gerry started to say the cork had *been* tight in the bottle because he had seen Keith put it in that morning when he had come to give Katy a hand with moving furniture out of the way of the painters. But the boy saw that explanations were useless, so he started out of the room with the milky rag. In so doing, he tripped over a foot held out *accidentally* in the aisle and went flat on his face.

"My, what a clumsy boy!" Miss Carpenter was out of patience with him and Gerry was glad to reach the safety of the hall.

The rest of the day passed without further accidents until Gerry left the building to go home. Several boys were lingering outside and he could see the heads of a few more peering around the corners of the building.

One of them came up to him and said with exaggerated

politeness, "Glad to meetcha, Gerry Berry Dirty Thirty. How is mama's little boy today?" And with that he pushed hard against him, knocking his lunchbox down on the cement of the playground along with his pencil box and books.

There was a crash from the lunchbox and some of the books landed in a mud puddle.

"You let me alone!" — cried Gerry, springing up. His hands were shaking as he started to pick up his possessions.

"Oh, mama's little man can get mad, can he?" And the boy gave Gerry another heavy push that sent him sprawling. Just then Paul Delasapio appeared on the run and pitched into the big fellow who was annoying Gerry. Whereupon other boys darted forward from every direction to pounce on Paul and Gerry. Fists began to fly when suddenly a small furry object hurtled into the fray. It was Dixie, growling and snarling, bristling and biting.

The fight stopped almost as soon as it began. Frightened by the aroused animal, the boys ran off as fast as they could. Dixie followed them and would have continued the fray in the next yard but Paul called him, picked him up and calmed him down with gentle words and pattings.

Gerry tucked in his new shirt that was now torn and dirty and picked up his things. He was mad. "They weren't fair! My father taught me it wasn't fair for more than one person to pick on another. He said sometimes you had to fight but

always to be fair. They ganged up on me, that's what they did."

"They sure did," agreed Paul, "or rather on us. It was about seven to two and some of them were bigger. But thanks to Dixie we won!"

"Aren't you right!" exclaimed Gerry with a grin, but he suddenly thought of something. "You know, he shouldn't have come all the way over here. How did he know the way? Think of all the busy streets he had to cross!"

"Yeah," said Paul. "I saw him crossing Cypress Street as I came along. He had his nose to the ground all the time. I guess he was following your trail."

"Oh, you good Dixie!" Gerry couldn't help but pat the little terrier even though he had crossed forbidden territory. "If you hadn't come along we would have been squashed!"

When Gerry got home, Mrs. Montgomery seemed to make light of the whole thing except Dixie's following the boy to school. "Don't worry about the boys too much, dear. You and Paul stick together and I don't think you'll have much trouble. But I must keep Dixie in the house and yard."

VI

GERRY'S SHIRT was a total loss and so was the Thermos bottle in his new lunchbox. Barbara and Gerry saw their mother frown slightly as she added these items to her next day's shopping list.

"What's the matter, Mom?" asked Barbara, whose first day at junior high school had been much more peaceful than Gerry's. "Are we running short again?"

Mrs. Montgomery looked up from her list. "Well, to tell the truth, dear, we are. I thought I had planned for everything but the painters and paperhangers say they hadn't figured on the ceilings being so high, so they had to buy more paint and paper, and that leak really cost quite a bit to repair."

"Why couldn't I work part-time like Katy?" asked Barbara. "Lots of the girls at school baby-sit and earn quite a bit of money. They say if you get the right kind of job — where you don't have to wash up a week's dishes or do all the ironing — you can get your homework done while the kids are asleep."

Instead of the "No, dear" that both children expected, Mrs. Montgomery asked, "Would you really like to, Barbara?"

"I certainly would, Mom," Barbara answered. "I think I might get a job tonight."

"Why don't you try it, then, dear?" suggested her mother. "And, you know, I believe I'll go over to the public library and see if I can't work in the children's room or at a school library. I was reading in the *Brookline Citizen* that they are very short of help and are even using people who have had no library training. After all, I know many of the good children's books from having read to you two so much."

"Aw, Mom, I don't like the idea of your working," objected Gerry. "Daddy wouldn't have liked that. Let *me* earn some money instead."

Mrs. Montgomery smiled at her son but shook her head. "No, someone has to stay home and take care of the place. You and Dixie have your job here and a very important one it is. Anyway they may not want me at the library."

But they were glad to get Mrs. Montgomery at the public library. She was assigned to evening hours at the desk in the main reading room, checking out books, until she had more experience.

The very first evening who should come up to the desk, book in hand, but Bill O'Brien! He blushed when he saw who the librarian on duty was.

"Gee, Missus, I didn't expect to see you here!"

"Hello, Bill," Mrs. Montgomery said. "I'm glad to see you

are a library customer. Let's see what you're taking out tonight."

Bill handed over the book sheepishly. It was *The Types and Volume of Turbo-jet Motors* by A. M. Shilling. "It ain't for me, ma'am. It's for my brother. He's going to night school in engineering so I have to get his books out for him."

"How about one for you, Bill?" Mrs. Montgomery inquired with a smile.

"Oh, me, reading don't agree with me!" he answered quickly. "Books is for the birds if you ask me."

"What do you do in your spare time, Bill?" the substitute librarian continued, unruffled.

"Oh, I have to take care of the baby like you know, and then I mostly hang around. What's the use of books? Reading don't get you nowhere," he insisted. "If I ever had any money, I wouldn't spend it on books. I'd get me a set of tools, a good set of carpenter tools. My uncle is a carpenter and he makes nice money. He lets me use his tools once in a while. But reading, it don't get you nowhere," he repeated.

Mrs. Montgomery could stand the abuse of the English language no longer. "It *doesn't* get you anywhere, Bill. Not *don't.*"

Bill laughed. *"Doesn't,* eh? Look, ma'am, it don't make

no difference how I say it as long as people understands me, see?"

"But, Bill — " Mrs. Montgomery was going to continue the argument when she suddenly had a different idea. "Bill, we have some fine books on carpentry. Wouldn't you like to look at one of them — just look?"

The boy hesitated.

"I'd like to see what they have myself," the librarian continued. "Come on, we'll find one right now." And before young Mr. O'Brien knew what was going on, he was being taught how to use the card index and soon found himself in front of a whole row of books on carpentry. Together they picked one out and then went through the routine of making out a library card for Bill, since he had never taken out a book before.

To Mrs. Montgomery's surprise Bill wrote his name and the necessary information with a very careful hand. "My, what nice, neat handwriting!" she said.

Bill looked pleased. "My uncle taught me a little draftsmanship," he explained. "And I can print good, too. See?" And he copied a line from a library notice on a piece of scrap paper.

"Oh, that's beautiful, Bill!" Mrs. Montgomery exclaimed. "Have you ever thought of draftsmanship as a career?"

But Bill's spell of co-operation was over. "What do I want

a career for? The army's going to get me in a coupla years. What's the use tryin' to learn anythin'? It don't make sense."

Mrs. Montgomery hesitated. She decided to bypass the larger problem for the smaller one. "It *doesn't* make sense, Bill. Not it *don't*."

Bill looked toward the door. "Okay, okay. It *doesn't*. Come on, snap it up. I gotta get out of here. I'm late to a movie now. My pal, he don't — "

"He *doesn't* — " cried Mrs. Montgomery, exasperated.

Suddenly Bill laughed. He understood persistence and determination and here it was in the woman before him.

"You see, Bill," continued Mrs. Montgomery, turning to an illustration in the carpentry book before her. "English is like carpentry. There is a word for every special use just as there is a tool for every special use. If you were going to put in a screw, you would use a screwdriver, not a chisel, wouldn't you?"

"You sure would! You could break your chisel with a stupid deal like that."

"All right," agreed Mrs. Montgomery. "There are places where you use *don't* and places where you use *doesn't,* and if you are given a fine set of tools like the English language you ought to use them right."

"Sure," agreed Bill, gathering up his books, "I'll try but sometimes it don't — I mean, it *doesn't* come too easy."

With that he left and Mrs. Montgomery sank back on her stool exhausted but smiling.

VII

BOTH THE BABY-SITTING and the library work were a success — so much so that Gerry was upset at not contributing anything himself. He thought and thought and finally decided to sell his English bicycle, a special one his father had brought over from London for him. After all, his mother wouldn't let him ride in their new neighborhood anyway because of the traffic, so why should he keep it when they needed the money?

He puzzled about how to dispose of it and finally decided to put a notice up on the Exchange Board in his school locker room. He hesitated when he thought that perhaps some of the boys who had picked on him might answer the notice, but he had had no more trouble since the first day, so he decided to take a chance.

He wheeled the bike around to a nearby gas station to find out what it was worth. The attendant was enthusiastic. "Brother, that's a sweet bike! I never saw a better. Special brakes, special gears, special saddle. I wish I could afford to buy it for my own boy but you ought to get seventy-five dollars for her. She must have cost a hundred and fifty."

That seemed like a lot of money to Gerry so he didn't put the price on his notice. It simply read:

SPECIAL ENGLISH BIKE FOR SALE
APPLY 42 WALNUT STREET BETWEEN 3 AND 5 P.M.

Those were the hours he knew his mother and sister would be working now and so would Katy.

That same day a dozen or so boys turned up at the Montgomery house to look at the bike. But none of them could offer more than ten dollars to pay for it. Gerry had enough sense not to sell it for that little and he was getting discouraged when along toward five o'clock an older boy appeared with a pack of newspapers over his back. He whistled when he saw the bicycle.

"Phew, a Raycroft Phantom! I never expected you'd have

one of those. I've wanted one all my life. What are you asking for it, kid?"

Gerry gulped. He knew now he couldn't get $75. He was pretty sure no one would pay him $50, so he decided to try to get what he could. "Twenty-five dollars," he whispered.

"Twenty-five dollars!" shouted the older boy with glee. "It's a deal, mister. I'll go right home and get the money! My name's Jack Taylor — I'll be right back."

He started to run out the drive but something made him stop and slowly retrace his steps.

"What are you selling it for, bud?" he asked, looking sternly at Gerry. "Does it really belong to you? It's a British racing bike, you know."

"Yes, I know," said Gerry miserably. "I'm selling it because we need the money. My sister and mother both work and earn money, but I can't because someone has to stay home. So I'm selling the bike for my share." He turned his face away to keep from showing his distress. He didn't want to sell his bike at all.

For a moment Jack Taylor didn't say anything. He just looked at the mournful huddle of boy and dog, for Dixie, always at hand when his master was in trouble, had come up and put his head in his lap.

"Listen, kid, I'm not going to buy your bike. It's worth three or four times what you're asking. I'm not that low.

60

You've got to earn your money some other way." Suddenly his face lit up. "Listen, I've got an idea. Why didn't I think of it before? I'm going to give up this paper route because there's a better job in the garage around the corner. Why don't you take it over? You're kinda little but I think you could do it okay. You'd have to go down in the tough part of this neighborhood but take that dog along and you'll be all right. I can see he'll stick right with you."

Gerry's face brightened and he leaped to his feet. "Could I? Oh, wouldn't that be wonderful! And I wouldn't have to sell my bike! Oh boy, oh boy!"

Jack grinned at his enthusiasm. "You won't earn too much right away but it'll mount up and you'll get a lot more than twenty-five dollars if you stick with it — and you'll still have your bike."

Gerry couldn't thank him enough and insisted he come in and have some of Katy's biscuits and jam.

"Jeepers, those are really biscuits!" the boy exclaimed. "Well, I'll be going. I'll talk to Mr. Gregg — he's the boss — and you'll have to make sure it's okay with your family. I'll come over tomorrow night, and if everything's all right I'll go over the route with you. And see that you have some more of those biscuits. That's really cool food!"

That night when Gerry told his mother about the paper route, she hesitated.

"Does this mean you'd go down to Fountain Square and the warehouse district?"

"I don't know," Gerry answered uncertainly. "I guess so. But this boy Jack Taylor said to take Dixie and I'd be all right. Or perhaps I could go on my bike?"

"No, son." His mother was firm on this point. "The throughway begins at Fountain Square and the traffic is terrible."

"Anyway," Barbara put in, "if the people are so tough down there, they might take your bike away from you."

Mrs. Montgomery looked at the big brown eyes of her son, fixed so imploringly upon hers. She knew he wanted to have a part in helping the family. "Let's try it. I honestly don't think this part of the city is as bad as some people say."

"You mean I can do it? Whoopee!" Gerry sprang up with joy. "Dixie, we've got a job! Or at least I hope we have!" The dog sprang up too and gave little short barks of glee. Together they rushed out of the house and tore up and down outside in senseless antics until it was time to go to bed.

VIII

THE NEXT NIGHT Jack Taylor appeared and reported he had fixed up with Mr. Gregg that Gerry should have the paper route. Jack ate one biscuit after another while Katy beamed at him and Mrs. Montgomery questioned him about the route. There were over seventy papers to deliver. Mr. Gregg threw them off his truck in two bundles at different places.

"It isn't so hard," said Jack, "once you get the hang of it. I've planned the route so you only cross the throughway twice. And if you just press the WALK light each time, and wait for it, you're safe enough. Cars have to stop for the red and yellow light."

As soon as Jack finished, and Katy had pushed half a dozen extra biscuits in his pockets, he and Gerry set out together on the route with Dixie close at their heels.

In two hours Gerry was back, full of enthusiasm for his new job. Dixie seemed to share it too, for he capered around the kitchen while the boy described the houses where he had to stop and the people he had talked to.

"They were nice, Mom," he said earnestly. "Most of the people who answered the bell patted Dixie and said hello to me. Once, at a third floor apartment, a pan came banging down the stairs after I rang and someone yelled at me but Jack said to think nothing of it. In that apartment the people throw pots and pans at each other for fun. That's a strange thing to do, isn't it, Mom?"

His mother laughed. "It certainly is. Was that the only place anything strange happened?"

The boy thought for a moment and then answered, "No, at another place a little boy came running downstairs and he was sort of crying and said his father had hit him but Jack said for me to mind my own business. So we just left the paper and went. Anyway I guess he's all right by now."

"He probably is," Mrs. Montgomery agreed although there was a startled look in her eyes.

"Praises be!" put in Katy, who had listened in on the

recital. "It's learning early he is. Now you do what this Jack fellow says. Mind your own business."

"Oh, I will," promised Gerry. "Nothing could happen to me with Dixie. They all like him."

And for a while nothing did happen to Gerry. He came back with a few tales of family squabbles and neighborhood fights but he also told of making many friends, mostly through Dixie. There was old Kevin Malloy, the shoemaker, who was too crippled to work any more and who sat in a chair by the window waiting eagerly for his evening paper. He put a patch on Gerry's overshoe one night when they stopped by in a hard rain. And there was Mrs. MacManus, who lived in a three-room flat with seven children. She always welcomed Gerry and Dixie and urged the boy and dog to stay and play with her jolly brood, one of whom was Gerry's age. She never failed to have something for them — a bit of candy or cake or a flower to take home to Gerry's mother, for Mr. MacManus worked on a big estate where they had a greenhouse.

"The poorer they are," said Gerry, "the more they want to give me things. I can't understand it."

His mother smiled. "Remember the Bible says, 'It is better to give than to receive.' People get real pleasure from sharing, no matter how little they have."

Gerry agreed. "They certainly do and are they nice to *me!*"

So all three of the Montgomerys were gainfully employed, and as winter began the old house seemed to radiate good spirits. Everyone would disappear in the morning, Gerry and Barbara to school, and Katy and Mrs. Montgomery to work. She had to be at the library when it opened now. Gerry would be home first, in the early afternoon, and would play around with Dixie until the newspaper truck came by about four o'clock and dropped the first bundle of papers at the front door. Then off would go boy and dog down the street, with Gerry lessening his load as he threw paper after paper onto front steps or pushed them in mailboxes.

After a week or so, he had memorized the route and knew without looking at his list just who his customers were. Dixie seemed to know too, and before long Gerry began to give the dog the rolled-up papers to take and drop on the porches or the front door steps while he pushed in those that had to be left in mailboxes.

All went well until the middle of December, when Gerry woke up one morning with a bad cold. He said nothing to his mother, who was hurrying to make the beds before she left for work. He went to school but felt hot and strange by afternoon when the first bundle of papers was thrown off the truck. He made his rounds, but on his arrival back at the house Katy cried:

"Will you look at the lad! He's as white as next week's wash!"

This brought his mother into the kitchen. She sized up the situation in a moment. "Oh, Gerry, you have the flu, don't you? So many children who come into the library have had it. Did you feel all right this morning?"

Gerry hung his head. "No, Mother, but I wanted to go to school and deliver my papers. And I thought all the time I might feel better."

His mother put a loving arm around him. "Let's not do any more talking. It's bed for you and I'll call the doctor right away."

"But the route!" cried Gerry. "What about my paper route?"

His mother thought that over. "Maybe Paul could do it — no, his mother told me yesterday *he* has the flu. Perhaps I could ask one of the children who come in to the library — I know, I'll ask Bill O'Brien. He has books that are due to-morrow. He might do it."

"You don't mean that O'Brien boy who was here the first day we came?" cried Katy. "Sure and he'll deliver the first ten and throw the rest away. He's a bad actor, that one."

"I'm not so sure, Katy," Mrs. Montgomery replied. "He's been coming to the library quite regularly. I think he wants to improve."

"By gorry, he has a long way to go!" objected Katy. "You can't tell me he'll change overnight."

"But he won't know where to go." Gerry was worried. "Wait, I still have that first list with all the addresses. He could go by that."

Barbara had been listening in. "Let me do it, Mother. I'd be glad to."

"No," said Mrs. Montgomery and Gerry at once. "Not in that district at night."

"Well," added Barbara, "you said Dixie knew all the stops. Together I should think Bill and Dixie could manage it."

"I think I'll call Mr. Gregg." Mrs. Montgomery started toward the telephone in the hall. "Other boys must have been sick before this. He'll know what we ought to do. Meanwhile, Gerry, you start getting to bed. We'll fix it somehow. Don't worry."

But Mr. Gregg said that it was up to Gerry to get his own substitute or pay for all the undelivered papers. So the next day Mrs. Montgomery waited with some concern for Bill O'Brien to appear in the library. When he did, she asked him if he could take the route.

"Me deliver papers down in Fountain Square?" he protested. "That's where I live. Why, the gang would bust their sides laughing at me. I wouldn't do that for a million bucks."

"Well, I certainly couldn't pay you a million bucks, Bill,"

said Mrs. Montgomery, smiling. "But Gerry has the flu, the doctor says, and so has Paul Delasapio. We really don't know any other boys well enough to ask them. Barbara and I can probably do it all right anyway. I think it might be fun."

Bill gasped. "You and Barbara! You can't go down there! Why, it'll be dark by the time you get there. Honest, Mrs. Montgomery, you just can't go. Things happen there after dark."

"We'll have Dixie, he'll protect us," said Mrs. Montgomery quietly. "I'm not afraid."

Bill looked at her with eyes as big as headlights. "So you're not afraid! Jeepers, ma'am, I'll do it rather than have you do it. But it's goin' to be awful hard. Those guys are goin' to give me the big laugh."

"Thanks a lot, Bill." Mrs. Montgomery impulsively held out her hand. They shook hands, and Bill blushed.

"That's all right, ma'am. My mother sometimes says I'm a lazy bum. But maybe this time I'll show her. Anyway it don't matter."

"It *doesn't* matter," corrected Mrs. Montgomery with a little giggle. "Anyway, I'm very grateful to you, Bill."

Bill looked up at her. Then he gave a friendly snort. "Okay. Doesn't. I'll be around tonight about five."

When Bill came at five, Barbara had the list ready. "Do you

want Dixie to go with you, Bill? He knows the route. He's used to delivering the papers where there's any walking to do."

Bill examined the list and then looked at the little dog, who didn't appear too friendly. Dixie remembered Bill and his quarrel with Gerry.

Bill hesitated. "I know the route all right but he might save some steps at that. And ya know, he has a real cool look to him. Maybe they wouldn't give me the big laugh if I had him. But how do ya know he'll come with me? He don't look like he wants any part of me."

And Dixie didn't. He refused to budge until Bill went out and picked up the bundle of newspapers and put them in the big newspaper bag. Then he watched him, puzzled.

Barbara commanded him to go with Bill but the dog stood undecided. He just didn't understand. And it wasn't until Barbara went upstairs and spoke to Gerry that anything happened.

Gerry in pajamas poked his head out the window and called to Dixie. "Go on, boy! Show Bill the way. Go on! I'm sorry I can't go. But you go. Be a good dog, Dixie. *Go!*"

And Dixie went. Head and tail down, he trotted after Bill O'Brien as if he were being punished.

All went well until they reached Fountain Square. There cars swirled around the traffic circle in the steady hum of rush-hour traffic. The wind was sharp and cold, the early

71

dark of winter had settled down, and the gloom was only partly cut by a few high-up neon lights and the illumination from some shabby storefronts. Boys just out of high school stood in knots in front of a vacant building while others lingered by tenement doors.

When Bill O'Brien and Dixie appeared, there was a universal hoot of laughter. "Cripes, look at Bill! Look at our little newsboy! Ain't he sweet?"

"Earnin' a livin' at last, Bill? When ya goin' to get your Cadillac?"

"Look, he has the pooch the little guy had. What a runty pooch! That size ain't good for nothin'. Where'd ya steal him, Bill?"

Bill called, "Take it easy, fellas," and tried to pay no attention. He was doing a good job, pushing papers in letter slots until it came Dixie's turn to carry a paper down an alley to a tiny secondhand shop. This he did, proudly and well, dropping it neatly up against the door just as it opened and a hand reached out into the cold breeze for the paper.

The boys thought this was great. They clapped each other on the shoulder and joked and laughed. Bill relaxed in the admiration they had for his temporary dog.

"How do ya do it, Bill? Lemme give it to him. Lemme do it, Bill," cried several.

So Bill showed them how he wadded up the paper. "Then you give it to him like this," he said as they came to another alley where Dixie made the delivery.

But just as Bill was going to give it to the dog, a youngster grabbed it, trying to show off. "Lemme have it. Let's see if he's any good. Here! Catch, Joe!" And he tossed it up in the air, intending to throw it to a boy who was lounging in a doorway nearby. His aim was poor, though, and a gust of wind took the paper and blew it across the sidewalk and then right out into the middle of the traffic.

Dixie had anxiously watched the fooling. He knew it was

his job to deliver that paper to the doorway down the alley. So when the paper was thrown, he went after it.

The first car missed him by swerving. But the driver of the second car didn't see him at all and hit him squarely in the side, the car passing over him and beyond before it stopped. There was a general yell, with a high scream from Bill, and all traffic stopped because of the pile-up.

The boy dropped his papers and, white-faced, made his way through the cars to the still, furry form on the cement. His hands were shaking as he bent to pick up the little dog. One of Dixie's legs stuck out strangely and blood was oozing from his mouth.

Bill was surrounded by boys when he again reached the sidewalk and the driver of the car had to push his way through a dense circle to reach the boy and the dog.

"Gee, fella, I just didn't see him! I'm sure sorry. Really I am. Is he — is he dead?"

"I dunno," Bill sobbed. "I guess so. He ain't moving. Nor nuthin. He ain't my dog but it's my fault."

A policeman shouldered his way through the crowd. "Too bad, boy. I'll take him. We have to give all dead dogs to the street department — that's the rules."

"Oh, no!" cried Bill. "I gotta take him back. I gotta take him back to Gerry and tell him what I done."

"No," said the officer. "Give him to me, Bill. They won't

want a dead dog back. Tell me who he belongs to and I'll go around and break it to them. It wasn't your fault. You don't have to tell them."

Bill straightened up. "I'm *going* to tell them. And I'm going to carry him back there, too."

The driver of the car broke in. "I'll give the boy a ride, officer. We'll take care of this. I think the thing to do is to take the dog to the Animal Rescue League first. They'll know if anything can be done for him and we can wait there for the family if he is dead. I'm very sorry. I have a couple of dogs of my own."

"Okay, have it your way," said the policeman. "But I wouldn't bother if I were you. Dogs get killed here all the time and we got it fixed that the street department takes 'em away."

It was a sad family that heard the news of the accident. Mrs. Montgomery and Barbara went right down to the Animal Rescue League but the young doctor wouldn't let them see Dixie.

"He's a mess, ma'am. He's still alive but he hasn't got much of a chance. His right front leg is broken and his ribs are crushed. Dr. Matson is going to operate, but if one of those ribs goes through the lungs, it's all over. We'll let you know how it comes out. He's a fine little dog."

Mrs. Montgomery hated to tell Gerry the news, but the white-faced little boy took it gamely. "Well, you could say he died doing his job, Mother. Daddy would say he was a good soldier." And he turned his face into the pillow.

"Yes, he would," agreed his mother, and in her heart she thought her son was a good soldier, too.

Later that night there came a little knock at the back door. Katy was alone in the kitchen and went to open it. When she saw Bill O'Brien she started to blast at him but one look at his dejected face and reddened eyes stopped her.

"So it's you, is it?" A not very smart question but all she could think of at the moment.

"Yeah," said Bill, slouching into the room. "I'm all you said I was. A punk. A real punk. You can sure give it to me now. Go ahead, say it. You can't make it any worse than it is."

For the first time in her life Katy was speechless. She gazed at the downhearted boy a good half minute before replying. "Well, you'll make a bad situation no better by dragging around here like a ghost. Here it is almost Christmas and you've made it a sad one for this family."

"I know it," answered Bill, staring into space. "It's all my fault. I'm a good-fer-nothin' just like my mother says."

Mrs. Montgomery came into the room then. She was

startled to see Bill, but when she saw the misery on his face, she went over and put her arms around him.

"Bill," she said, "it wasn't your fault. We don't blame you. You must believe that. It could have happened right out in front of this house."

"But it didn't!" Bill had trouble keeping his voice steady. "I'll make it up to Gerry, ma'am. Really I will, believe me. And I'll do the paper route until he gets well. And I'll do it right, too."

"Thank you, Bill. Now let's go and cheer up Gerry. And

I've just remembered — we're having a Christmas party Saturday. Would you come?"

Bill raised his head in surprise. "You want *me?* Even after what I done?"

Mrs. Montgomery patted his shoulder. "I certainly do. And I was hoping you might help me make a stand for the Christmas tree. There will be lots of things to do."

"Oh, I sure would like to help you!" cried Bill, his voice still a little uneven. "I'll be here."

"And bring that red-headed sister of yours," put in Katy. "I could do with a baby in my kitchen again. Sure, and children grow up too fast, they do. Look at you, you big lout, I'll bet even you were a cute baby."

Bill managed a teasing smile. "My mother says I was — but she sure has changed her mind since!"

IX

THE MONTGOMERYS decided to ask all their new friends to the Christmas party. They were still very sad about Dixie, who was lingering between life and death, but they had reconciled themselves to the worst because Dr. Matson had said the chances for the little dog were so slim. So they were determined to try to celebrate Christmas as they always had.

Gerry was up on his feet after his illness and Mrs. Montgomery had been given a week's holiday from the library to be with her family.

"Let's ask the Delasapios," said Mrs. Montgomery. "And who else? You children can ask anyone you want. We really are doing very nicely about expenses now so let's have a real party."

"I'd like to have Dot and Peggy from school," said Barbara. "And, Mother, do you suppose I could ask the family I've been baby-sitting for? Mrs. Dubinsky is so nice. She works at night and her husband works in the daytime but she said she would have Saturday off. And they could put the baby to bed in my room."

"Wonderful!" agreed Mrs. Montgomery. "And I'd like to have two of the librarians — they've helped me so much. One has a husband who works for the Edison Company and the other lives with her father. I do hope they all have the evening free."

"How about me?" asked Gerry. "I have a lot of friends I want you to meet. There's Mr. Malloy, and do you suppose we could have the MacManuses? Golly, there's nine of them!"

"Natch," Barbara replied and her mother nodded enthusiastically. "Now, how about Katy?"

"Katy can speak for herself," came a voice from the kitchen, and Katy appeared around the pantry door. "It's Mr. Dillon and his wife I'd like to have in this. She's been ailing and I think she's purely lonesome for some children. Hers are all grown up and moved to California. It sounds as if she might find plenty here. Would that be all right, Mrs. Montgomery?"

"It surely would." Mrs. Montgomery had a happy flush to

her cheeks and looked more like her own cheerful self than at any time since her husband had died.

"And," added Katy with decision, "I think it's the place for a good O'Dean Irish stew."

"And a good MacPhersen Scottish brew," put in Keith, who had just come in, looking very commanding and pleased in his coveralls with *MacPhersen Service* sewed in red letters on the front.

"How about it, Keith? Would you like to add some friends to our numbers?" asked Mrs. Montgomery.

"I think not," said Keith. "The boys will be busy at the station. But we *will* have an unknown extra at your party. Jane and I are expecting a baby at last. He will be there — kind of quiet this time — but next year you will have to count him in." The big Scotsman stood up, proud and plain.

"Oh Keith, how wonderful! My husband would have been so pleased." Mrs. Montgomery and Keith had a warm handshake and then they all put their heads together on plans for the party.

The day of the party was bright, cold and clear. A light snow had fallen the night before and Gerry was out sweeping the sidewalk soon after breakfast. Barbara and Mrs. Montgomery gathered evergreens to make a wreath from the ancient trees around the place. There were pine, hemlock, spruce and

dark, glossy yew, and Barbara found some bittersweet in a secluded place. That and berries from the barberry hedge made a sharp spot of color against the green.

Mrs. Montgomery showed them how to fasten the branches and berries on an old barrel hoop they discovered in the barn. She used fine wire and made the whole wreath firm with it before adding a big red satin bow at the top.

"My mother taught me how to do this years ago," she said, "and I guess that is one reason why I like old-fashioned Christmas decorations. I know the modern silver and blue arrange-

ments are very pretty but they just don't mean Christmas to me somehow."

The children nodded in agreement, and when she hung the wreath on the tall mahogany front door they all breathed "Ah-h-h" in satisfaction.

As they finished their wreath hanging, Bill O'Brien strode up the walk. "Hi, folks!" he greeted them. "I've found just the thing for the Christmas tree." They had all gone to purchase the tree two days before at a roadside stand. It was a perfect little spruce — small, fat and healthy-looking.

"My old man was lookin' for spare parts for his car at the dump yesterday and I went along," Bill continued. "Look at what I found!" He held up two hunks of rusty machinery.

They all tried to look enthusiastic but failed.

"Oh, all right, all right," said Bill good-naturedly. "Wait till you see them in action."

He disappeared in the direction of the living room where he had dragged the tree. Soon there came sounds of sawing and hammering mixed with a few groans and choice words which made Keith MacPhersen smile as he went by the door.

Keith had made the rounds of the house with his stepladder and an armful of Christmas decorations. He had wound the long mahogany stair rail with a green festoon. A big bunch of mistletoe hung over the library door and he had laid logs for open fires in all four of the marble fireplaces. Mr. Mac-Manus had sent a big box of red roses and these Keith had lovingly arranged in a white alabaster vase they had found in the attic. The Scotsman loved flowers and decorations and he stepped lightly and admiringly through all the rooms of the house to check them for the last time before he left for the kitchen and the concoction of his Scottish brew.

Soon he and Katy could be heard joking and laughing out there and the smell of rich, delicious stew blended on the air with the cinnamon, saffron and other spices of the brew. Ginger cookies and mince pie gave off their heady odors too and soon the old house was rich with the tantalizing aroma of Christmas.

Mrs. Montgomery and the children both cried "Ah-h-h!" when they came in the door and were glad that Katy had ready deep bowls of split pea soup and a fresh chocolate cake to ease their hunger which had been sharpened by the crisp outdoors and the smell of party wonders to come. Bill came from the living room to join them but disappeared homeward after a while to get ready for the party.

Soon people all began arriving at once and there was much introducing and handshaking. Everyone was enchanted by the old house which had come so thoroughly to life. The children gathered around the crackling fire in the dining room, where Katy served them cups of cocoa with big dollops of whipped cream on top. In the library Keith ladled out his Scottish brew and even Mr. Malloy and Mr. MacManus allowed that it wasn't bad to taste even though they *did* make better mixtures in Ireland!

Soon Bill arrived and conferred in whispers with Mrs. Montgomery. Then he went outside and got a clumsy-looking sack which he carried quickly down cellar. When he came back, he slid behind the big mahogany doors into the living room and shut them after him. But in a few minutes he was out again, beckoning to Mrs. Montgomery.

She then rose and said, "Please won't you all join us in the living room, where we have a few surprises."

She swung open the big doors and young and old flooded into the beautiful high room. The old crystal chandelier had been polished and reflected in its hundreds of droplets the candlelight from the candelabra and the lively fire in the fireplace. The old mahogany furniture sparkled too with newly applied polish and seemed to smile as if it realized that it was part of a very special party.

Everything seemed to fit into a lovely picture, but the gayest bit was the fat little spruce tree, all decorated and lighted up, which slowly revolved on a pedestal at the far end of the room.

Mrs. Montgomery gasped. "Oh, Bill, did you get the revolving pedestal from the dump? It's wonderful!"

"Yes, ma'am," said Bill, his face flushing with pleasure.

"But wait until you see what else I found. Paul helped find it and we fixed it up at his father's place. Paul said maybe it might not be right for tonight but I thought it was pretty. And — " he hesitated — "I kinda thought you would too."

With that he bent down and pressed a little lever in the side of the pedestal. It continued to revolve but soon a few notes of music tinkled out on the air and finally it was obvious that the tree was spinning around merrily to the tune "Anchors Away!"

Mrs. Montgomery laughed wholeheartedly as did the other grownups. Mrs. Delasapio seemed especially amused.

"Oh, thank you, Bill!" Mrs. Montgomery exclaimed. "It's an old-fashioned music box. I've always loved them. You and Paul have been so thoughtful — thank you."

"Gee, Bill," said Gerry, looking at the tree as it turned in time to the song, "that's cool. I wish you'd take me to that dump sometime."

"I sure will," said Bill.

"And now, my friends," said Mrs. Montgomery, "let's all join in a few Christmas carols. Mrs. Delasapio is going to play for us and lead the singing. What shall we start with?"

One of the children's librarians said, "I always like to start Christmas with 'Holy Night.' "

"Oh, Mother!" cried Gerry. "That's the song your dog

88

used to sing to. Oh, Mother, I wish Dixie were here to sing. I miss him so much."

"I know you do, dear," said Mrs. Montgomery gently, "but let's try not to be sad this Christmas."

"All right," agreed Gerry and soon joined the guests as they sang "Holy Night" and many other carols, led by Mrs. Delasapio's lovely voice. The high sopranos of the children blended with the lower notes of the adults and those old songs were never more heartily sung than that winter night in the old Brookline house.

When the carol singing was over, Mrs. Montgomery invited them all into the dining room, where Katy's stew, salad, cookies and pie were awaiting them.

They were about to troop in together when Bill O'Brien spoke up again. "Please, ma'am, there is one thing we all want to say before we eat. I mean I speak for everybody in this room — the Delasapios, the MacManuses, Mr. Malloy and lots of others. You've been nice to us and we're so glad you're here and we're so sorry about what happened to Dixie that we got you a little present. Wait a minute — " and he turned and ducked into the kitchen and slammed down the cellar stairs. He was back in a moment with a strange bundle of fuzz. When set on its feet it turned out to be a little puppy, half cocker spaniel and half something else. Anyway he was as cute as could be and seemed to know it.

"It's for Gerry," said Bill, mumbling his words, "I know he isn't a very fancy dog. He came from a pet store over in Dorchester. But maybe he might turn *in* to be a very good dog, if you know what I mean."

Everyone laughed, as Gerry cried, "He's wonderful, Bill, just wonderful!" And Mrs. Montgomery asked, "What's his name?"

"Well, Mrs. Montgomery," and again Bill blushed. "I hope you won't mind this. You remember trying so hard to make me talk right? Well, his name is Duzzy, short for Doesn't!"

A roar of laughter went up at this, especially from Gerry, Barbara and Mrs. Montgomery. Just then Keith stepped out of the group and came back in a moment with this message. "Telephone, Mrs. Montgomery. I think he said his name was Dr. Matson."

Mrs. Montgomery's heart sank as did everyone else's in the room. Why did the bad news about Dixie have to come at their Christmas party? A hush fell on the group until Mrs. Montgomery returned. Her pale face could mean either good or bad news but everyone feared for the worst.

They were wrong. In a small voice, Mrs. Montgomery declared, "We've had good news. Dixie is going to live. Dr. Matson says that during the last few hours he has opened his eyes and looked around and for the first time seems interested in living and eating."

"Oh, Mother!" Gerry gave one great leap at his mother.

Everyone exclaimed with pleasure, especially Bill O'Brien, but he suddenly remembered the warm handful of puppy that had sat himself down by the hearth and was gazing into the living room fire for all the world like an old hand of a house dog: Duzzy.

Bill turned to Gerry and said softly, "I guess you won't be wanting this little mutt now Dixie is coming back. I wish I could take him but my mother won't have any animals."

"Oh, no!" cried Gerry. "Don't take him away. Let us keep him for you. Let's see — it will be Duzzy of Dorchester and Dixie of Dover! That's a slick combination, don't you think?"

Everybody agreed! It somehow made this Christmas complete.